Dear Parents:

Congratulations! Your child is taking the first steps on an exciting journey. The destination? Independent reading!

STEP INTO READING® will help your child get there. The program offers five steps to reading success. Each step includes fun stories and colorful art or photographs. In addition to original fiction and books with favorite characters, there are Step into Reading Non-Fiction Readers, Phonics Readers and Boxed Sets, Sticker Readers, and Comic Readers—a complete literacy program with something to interest every child.

Learning to Read, Step by Step!

Ready to Read Preschool–Kindergarten
• big type and easy words • rhyme and rhythm • picture clues
For children who know the alphabet and are eager to begin reading.

Reading with Help Preschool–Grade 1
• basic vocabulary • short sentences • simple stories
For children who recognize familiar words and sound out new words with help.

Reading on Your Own Grades 1–3
• engaging characters • easy-to-follow plots • popular topics
For children who are ready to read on their own.

Reading Paragraphs Grades 2–3
• challenging vocabulary • short paragraphs • exciting stories
For newly independent readers who read simple sentences with confidence.

Ready for Chapters Grades 2–4
• chapters • longer paragraphs • full-color art
For children who want to take the plunge into chapter books but still like colorful pictures.

STEP INTO READING® is designed to give every child a successful reading experience. The grade levels are only guides; children will progress through the steps at their own speed, developing confidence in their reading.

Remember, a lifetime love of reading starts with a single step!

Copyright © 2024 Disney Enterprises, Inc. and Pixar. All rights reserved. Published in the United States by Random House Children's Books, a division of Penguin Random House LLC, 1745 Broadway, New York, NY 10019, and in Canada by Penguin Random House Canada Limited, Toronto, in conjunction with Disney Enterprises, Inc.

Step into Reading, Random House, and the Random House colophon are registered trademarks of Penguin Random House LLC.

Visit us on the Web!
rhcbooks.com

Educators and librarians, for a variety of teaching tools, visit us at RHTeachersLibrarians.com

ISBN 978-0-7364-4444-6 (trade) — ISBN 978-0-7364-9047-4 (lib. bdg.)
ISBN 978-0-7364-4445-3 (ebook)

Printed in the United States of America

10 9 8 7 6 5 4 3 2 1

Random House Children's Books supports the First Amendment and celebrates the right to read.

DISNEY·PIXAR

INSIDE OUT 2

Riley's New World

adapted by Kathy McCullough
illustrated by the Disney Storybook Art Team

Random House 🏠 New York

Riley Andersen

Riley is officially a teenager—
which means big changes!
She got braces, outgrew
her favorite shirt, and will
soon be entering high school.
Riley doesn't realize that even
bigger changes are still to come.

Grace and Bree

Luckily, Riley's two best friends
are always by her side.
Grace is a little goofy,
while Bree is the quiet one.

Grace and Bree share
Riley's love of ice hockey,
and together they help
their team win
the Junior League
championship!

Valentina Ortiz

Riley's big win earns her an
invitation to hockey camp,
where she meets Valentina Ortiz.

Valentina is the cool, confident
captain of the varsity hockey team
at Riley's high school.
Val got on the varsity team
when she was just a freshman!

Riley doesn't know it, but she has
another team close by,
helping her manage
the ups and downs of life.

Five Emotions live and work
in Riley's Headquarters.
Their job is to protect
Riley's Sense of Self.

11

Joy

Joy keeps things running
smoothly in Headquarters.
She inspires Riley to see the
bright side of any situation.
Joy helped tackle big
challenges during Riley's first
twelve years, and she is proud that
Riley ended up happy and hopeful.
Joy is sure she can help Riley
succeed in her teen years, too!

Sadness

Although Sadness sometimes
puts a damper on a good mood,
this Emotion keeps Riley
in touch with her heart.
Sadness often doubts herself,
but she can always be counted on
to save the day when Riley and
the other Emotions need her help.

Anger

Anger will blow his stack
if things aren't going well
for Riley.
But his hotheaded focus
also helps Riley stay strong and
confident when she needs to be—
like in the final seconds of a
championship hockey game!

Fear

Fear might be overprotective
of Riley, but keeping her from
getting hurt is his job!
Fear is always watching out for
anything that might harm Riley.
He works to steer her clear of
danger and keeps her prepared
to face any problem—safely.

Disgust

Disgust is ready to help Riley

conquer being a teen.

In fact, she's been training

for this moment most of

Riley's life.

After all, Disgust has always

been the one to alert Riley

to anything cringey, gross,

or uncool.

But these five are not the only
Emotions who plan to help guide
Riley through her teen years.

Joy and the others are surprised
when four new Emotions arrive
at Headquarters!

Anxiety

Anxiety has big plans for Riley!
She's an expert at predicting
everything that could
go wrong in Riley's future.
Anxiety believes her job is to
make sure Riley does whatever
it takes to be successful,
even if that means changing
her Sense of Self.

Envy

To Envy, there is always
something better to do,
better to be, or better to have.
Envy helps Riley aim high and
improve herself and her life.
But sometimes Envy makes Riley
forget to be grateful for
what she already has.

Embarrassment

Embarrassment doesn't like
being the center of attention.
But it's hard not to notice him.
Embarrassment keeps Riley humble.
And even though he'd rather
hide in his hoodie, he's always
willing to help the other Emotions
do what's best for Riley.

Ennui

Ennui's name means "bored,"
and that's how she usually feels.
She can't be bothered to get
off the sofa to do her job.
She uses a phone app instead!
Ennui keeps Riley's enthusiasm
under control by prompting her
to scoff, shrug, and act like she
doesn't care—even if she does.

Joy and Anxiety have different ideas about how to guide Riley through her teen years. But together they realize Riley needs all nine Emotions to help her become her best self yet.